PUFFIN BOOKS

THE MARZIPAN PIG

The poor marzipan pig is stuck behind a sofa. No one heeds his lonely cries for help. Then a greedy mouse gobbles him up and is overwhelmed by a feeling of loneliness and yearning for love. So an extraordinary chain of events is set in motion, featuring an owl, a hibiscus and a mouse dressed in a pink frock! This charming, bitter-sweet tale of love is exquisitely illustrated by Quentin Blake.

Russell Hoban was born in Pennsylvania in 1925. He was in the US infantry during the war and afterwards lived in New York, where he had a variety of jobs. In 1967 he turned to writing full-time. His books in Puffin include *Harvey's Hideout*, *Bread and Jam for Frances*, *Dinner at Alberta's* and *The Mouse and his Child*. He now lives in London.

Another book by Russell Hoban

THE MOUSE AND HIS CHILD

RUSSELL HOBAN

THE
MARZIPAN
PIG

Illustrated by
QUENTIN BLAKE

PUFFIN BOOKS

PUFFIN BOOKS

Published by the Penguin Group
27 Wrights Lane, London w8 5tz, England
Viking Penguin Inc., 40 West 23rd Street, New York, New York 10010, USA
Penguin Books Australia Ltd, Ringwood, Victoria, Australia
Penguin Books Canada Ltd, 2801 John Street, Markham, Ontario, Canada l3r 1b4
Penguin Books (NZ) Ltd, 182–190 Wairau Road, Auckland 10, New Zealand

Penguin Books Ltd, Registered Offices: Harmondsworth, Middlesex, England

First published by Jonathan Cape Ltd 1986
Published in Puffin Books 1988
1 3 5 7 9 10 8 6 4 2

Made and printed in Great Britain by
Richard Clay Ltd, Bungay, Suffolk

There was nothing to be done for the marzipan pig. He fell behind the sofa and that was that. No one had seen him fall and no one knew where he was. He shouted, "Help!" but no one heard him. Night came, and morning, and there he still was.

"One would think they'd miss me," he said after a day or two. "One would think they'd look for me."

Perhaps they missed him and perhaps they looked for him but he was never found. Days passed and he sweated as marzipan will. He grew swarthy with the dust that settled on the glistening pinkness of him.

By day he listened to footsteps and voices that never came near him. Through the nights the street lamp shone outside the window and he waited in the dark behind the sofa listening to the ticking of the clock and the striking of the hours and the hooting of the owl on the common.

"There is," he said, "such sweetness in me!" No one heard him. He heard the rain beyond the window and the hiss of tyres on the street but no one came for him. Day after day he waited as the months went by. "I am growing hard," he said, "and

bitter. What a waste of me!"

One night he heard a gnawing sound behind the skirting board. "Help is coming," said the pig. He listened and he listened. Every night the gnawing sound came closer.

"Friends unknown to me have heard of my disappearance and are coming to the rescue," said the pig. "No doubt there'll be a big celebration when they find me. Crackers and party hats and probably a cake with pink icing. Perhaps I'll be stood on top of the cake and asked to make a speech."

He began to think of the speech he would make. "Dear friends," he said, "having spent long months in solitude behind the sofa, I speak to you tonight of . . ."

"Sweetness," said a voice behind him.

"Who's that?" said the pig.

It was a mouse. She was nibbling at him. "You're sweet," she said.

"There was a time when I was sweet," said the pig, "but I have known such . . ."

"Sweetness, sweetness, sweetness," murmured the mouse, and she ate him up entirely.

After eating the pig the mouse dozed for a time behind the sofa. When the clock struck three she woke up. "I wonder what that pig was going to say?" she said. "I couldn't stop eating him but now I wish I'd listened." In her were a craving and a sadness she had never known before.

"I'm so alone," she said. "It's so quiet here." She listened and she listened to the ticking of the clock. She watched the moving glimmer of the pendulum in the dim light from the street lamp. "Speak to me," she said to the clock, "do."

"Night," said the clock. "Only, only, only night."

"Surely there's more?" said the mouse.

"Lonely night," the clock said. "Lonely, lonely, lonely night."

"Ah! The loneliness!" the mouse said. "That's what the pig was going to say, I'm sure of it."

"Minutes, hours, days and years," the clock said.

"You have a kind face," said the mouse. "Make me happy! Love me, do!"

"Half-past three," said the clock, and went on ticking.

"You've more than that to say to me," said the mouse. She gnawed a little hole in the case of the clock and crept inside it so that she could be closer to the moving glimmer of the pendulum. She sat there listening to the ticking and the striking of the hours but the clock would tell her nothing but the time.

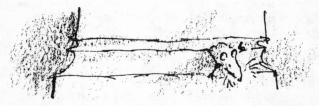

In the morning the mouse came out of the clock and went back behind the skirting board. But she came back that night and every night and sat inside the clock and waited for the clock to say it loved her. But the clock would tell her nothing but the time.

One night she didn't come back. The clock struck
midnight and there was no mouse. Half-past twelve
and one o'clock and still no mouse. While the lamp
shone outside the window he struck all the hours
and half-hours of the night but the mouse never
came. The little warm place where she used to sit
was cold and empty.

By day the clock could feel himself coiled tight
inside and waiting for the night. By night he felt the
empty place inside him as he waited for the day to
come. The next time he was wound his spring broke
and his ticking stopped and time went on without
him.

The owl in the plane tree on the common was sitting where he always sat on Thursday nights, and it was raining. He was looking at the row of houses opposite the common when he saw a mouse come out from under the front door of No. 6.

The owl swooped down in silence through the rain and caught the mouse. He flew back up to the plane tree and ate the mouse, then he sat staring through the rain and he thought new thoughts.

"Love," said the owl. "Love, love, love!" he
shouted to the rain. "I'm in love," he said more
quietly. He looked down at the street and saw the
violet glow of a taxi meter. Slowly the taxi puttered
black and shining up the street, and in it was the
meter violet-glowing in the dark.

"You!" said the owl. "I love you!"

On the taxi's roof the amber light lit up and said,
"FOR HIRE."

"For ever!" said the owl. He swooped down on
the taxi and landed on the bonnet with a thump. The
bonnet was slippery with the rain, the owl slid on
his tail till the windscreen stopped him.

When the driver saw the owl's feet staring at him he stopped the taxi and rolled down the window. The owl stood up and looked in at the meter. "I love you," he said.

"FOR HIRE," said the meter.

The taxi driver couldn't understand what the owl was saying. He thought the owl wanted to ride in the taxi. "I don't think you've got any money," he said.

"Who?" said the owl.

"You," said the driver. "Money. You know what money is?"

"Who?" said the owl.

"You," said the driver. "Money." He took a handful of coins from his pocket and showed them to the owl.

"Ooh," said the owl.

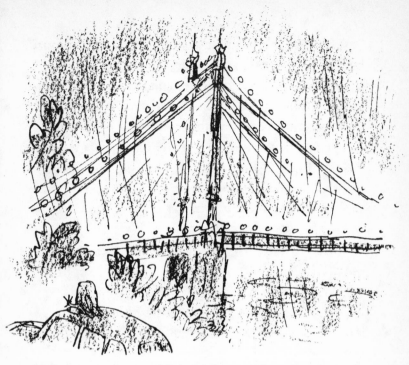

"That's money," said the driver. "No money, no ride." He started up the taxi and off he went. The owl flew up to the roof of the taxi and sat on top of the amber light.

The taxi driver drove to the cab stand by the Albert Bridge. The bridge was all lit up and shining in the rain. "Love!" said the owl. "Everything is bright for me!"

A lady came walking by. She was carrying a small handbag. The owl knew there was money in handbags. He swooped down and snatched it from her. He flew back to the taxi and dropped the bag on the bonnet. He looked in through the windscreen at the meter. "I love you," he said.

"FOR HIRE," said the meter.

"Stop, thief!" said the lady.

The driver gave the handbag back to the lady. He said to the owl, "You can't do that."

"Who?" said the owl.

"You," said the driver. "If you want a ride that badly, I'll give you one. But you'll have to pay me back some time, and not by stealing. Get in."

The driver opened the door and the owl perched on the back of the front seat by the meter. The driver started the meter and they drove off.

"I love you so much!" said the owl to the meter. "How much do you love me?"

"25p," said the meter.

"Love me more," said the owl.

"30p," said the meter.

"More and more!" said the owl.

"35p," said the meter. "40, 45."

"Yes," said the owl, "that's how it is. More and more and ever more. I am so happy with the lovely violet glow of you!"

"50p," said the meter as the cab pulled up at the cab stand by the bridge again. The driver stopped the taxi and turned off the lights. The meter went dark.

"Light up again," said the owl. "Tell me again how much you love me."

"That's it for tonight," said the driver. "Now it's time for trumpet practice."

"Who?" said the owl.

"Me," said the driver. He took a trumpet out of its case, climbed into the back seat, put his feet up on the back of the front seat, and began to play *When The Saints Come Marching In*.

"Speak to me," said the owl to the taxi meter. "Glow violet and lovely again."

The meter stayed dark and the driver kept playing his trumpet.

"This isn't fair," said the owl to the meter. "What have I done?" He jumped out of the taxi and danced with rage on the pavement. Without noticing it, he began to dance in time to the music. "What have I done, what have I done, what have I done to make you dark?" he hooted in time with the trumpet.

A man walking by threw 10p on the pavement by the owl.

"I want to see you glowing violet, I want to see your light again!" hooted the owl, still in time with the trumpet.

Another 10p dropped on the pavement.

"Nobody ever threw money before," said the driver. "You've got talent."

"Who?" said the owl.

"You," said the driver. "Keep singing and dancing. When you've made 50p you can have another ride."

"I want to see her glowing violet!" hooted the owl.

"That's it," said the driver. "Just carry on like that." And he went on playing his trumpet.

When the owl had 50p the driver started the taxi and the meter lit up again.

"Love!" said the owl. "You've come back to me!" And off they drove in the rain.

Under the plane tree where the owl had eaten the mouse there grew up a little pink flower. A passing bee noticed the flower and buzzed over to it. The bee sipped a little of the nectar.

"Different," said the bee. "Interesting." It sipped a little more. "Marzipan," it said. It sipped some more, and grew a little dizzy. "I've been working too hard," said the bee. "That's what it is." It stopped buzzing and sat down to rest.

The day was warm, the breeze was mild, the District Line trains rumbled past on the far side of the common and the bee fell asleep.

When the bee woke up it was dark. The houses standing opposite the common and the trains that rumbled past it were all lit with golden windows. The street lamps showed their globes of bluish light; footsteps and shadowy figures passed on the pavement. There was a full moon over the trees; there was a smell of honey-suckle in the air.

The bee looked up at the moon. "No sun," said
the bee. "I can't possibly find my way home without
the sun to go by. I'll have to stay in town tonight."

The bee flew up over the street lamps and past the
top-floor windows of the houses. At No. 6 a
window was open, and the bee saw the face of a
pinky-orange hibiscus looking round the edge of the
window-frame.

The bee flew into the room and saw that the hibiscus was growing out of a pot that stood on top of a bookshelf about a foot and a half to one side of the window. The stem of the plant leant to the window and curved up gracefully so that the flower could look out.

The bee flew round the flower and hovered in the darkness of the room, smelling the pinky-orange perfume of the hibiscus and looking at the light from the street lamp shining through her leaves and petals.

"Seen enough?" said the hibiscus.

"I'm sorry," said the bee. "I didn't mean to be rude." It flew round to the front where the flower could see it.

"You're not a gentleman, are you?" said the hibiscus.

"No," said the bee, "and I'm not a lady either. I'm just a worker."

"Never mind," said the hibiscus. "We can't all be posh."

"I might have been a Queen," said the bee.

"Oh yes," said the hibiscus, "and I might have been the Duchess of Gloucester but I'm not."

"You've gone to a lot of trouble to look out of that window," said the bee.

"That's not me, that's the plant," said the hibiscus. "The plant stays but the flowers come and go. Now I've had my turn. Tomorrow morning I'll be lying on the floor all crumpled like a dress thrown down after a dance."

The bee didn't say anything.

"At least I've got a full moon for my last night," said the hibiscus. "That's something. I wish I could have music." She began to hum in a high tinkly voice. "They play records here sometimes but they're out tonight. It's getting colder, isn't it?" She drew her thin and pinky-orange petals in a little. "So cold," she said, and wrapped her petals closer round her.

"I can't even sing for you," said the bee. "I can do a honey-dance though. Shall I dance for you?"

"Oh yes!" said the hibiscus. "Dance for me, do! Do it on the window sill so I can see you and the moon together."

"This is the dance that tells where the sweetest nectar is," the bee said. "It means, 'Sweet, sweet, so sweet! Sweet, sweet, this way!'"

"Sweet, sweet, so sweet!" murmured the hibiscus as the bee danced by the light of the street lamp and the trains rumbled past the common under the sinking moon. "Sweet, sweet, this way!"

As the bee danced it gave off the faintest scent of marzipan that mingled with the pinky-orange perfume of the hibiscus.

"Sweet, sweet!" whispered the hibiscus. She drew her petals tightly round her and drooped towards the sinking moon. "Fly away now for the honey," she said to the bee. "Fly so I can see you flying against the last of the yellow moon."

"I wish I could have been a gentleman for you," said the bee, and it flew off towards the golden passing windows of the District Line and the last of the yellow moon.

The upstairs mouse at No. 6 had watched the hibiscus plant in the front bedroom for a long time. She had seen the showy flowers one after another bloom and shrivel and fall to the floor. She used to sit behind the skirting board thinking how she would go about it if she were a hibiscus flower. Sometimes when there was no one in the bedroom she would run out on to the carpet and strike hibiscus poses in front of the full-length glass.

"Poor silly things," she used to say to herself. "They're pretty enough but they have no grasp. One after another they make the same mistake: they let go. The thing to do is, once you've bloomed, hold on. Just simply hold on and don't let go. There one is and there one stays. Yes," she said as she turned round and round in front of the glass, "and I've certainly got more of a figure than any of them, though I say it myself."

One morning the mouse came out of the hole in the skirting board and saw a hibiscus flower lying crumpled and closed on the floor. For a few moments the mouse paced back and forth clasping and unclasping her paws. She stopped in front of the glass and looked at herself. "Today is the day," she said.

The mouse went to the sewing-basket and got a needle and thread. She stripped the pinky-orange petals from the crumpled hibiscus flower and out of them she made herself a stylish little frock.

"Chic," she said, turning round and round in front of the glass. "Either one has it or one hasn't."

"Now, then," said the mouse. She looked up at
the flower pot on top of the bookshelf. The graceful
curving stem of the plant leant out to the open
window and its leaves all quivered in the autumn
breeze.

The mouse climbed up the bookshelf and into the
flower pot. She carefully began to work her way up
the long curving stem of the hibiscus plant so that
she could take her place as a flower on the end of it.

"The thing to do is simply hold on," she said, but
the stem drooped and swayed with her weight, the
tight frock made her clumsy, she lost her grip and
fell out of the window.

The postman was just coming to the steps of No. 6 when the mouse plummeted into his post-bag. The postman already had the letters for No. 6 in his hand. He hadn't seen the mouse fall into the bag and he didn't put his hand into the bag until he was coming down the steps.

When the mouse saw the postman's great big hand coming at her she was very frightened. She bit his finger, and not knowing what else to do, she kept her teeth closed on the postman's finger and held on.

"Ow!" yelled the postman. He flung up his arm and the mouse shot up into the air like a rocket.

The mouse flew through the air into the plane tree on the edge of the common. It was a Monday morning, and the owl in the plane tree was dozing where he always dozed on Monday mornings.

The mouse thudded into the owl and knocked him off the branch he was sitting on. "Oof!" said the owl as he went off the branch with his eyes still shut and his wings folded.

30

"Oof!" said the owl again as he hit the next branch ten feet down.

"Love!" shouted the owl as he grabbed the branch and opened his eyes. "Love has hit me like a thud in the stomach! Love, love, where are you? Who, who, who is it?"

He looked up and saw the mouse looking down at him. Not knowing what else to do, she was holding on to the branch the owl had fallen from.

"Love!" shouted the owl. "The breakfast of your eyes!" He meant to say "brightness".

The owl flew up and the mouse ran down the tree-trunk as fast as she could, across the street, up the steps, under the door,

and into No. 6.

Once inside the front door she stopped to catch her breath. "What a morning this has been," she said.

The mouse looked up at the letter basket on the door and saw among the letters a small brown-paper packet. She was very fond of brown-paper packets. "What harm can it do to look?" she said.

The mouse climbed up into the letter basket. "There's a corner of that packet just the least little bit torn open," she said. She sniffed the open corner and smelt something sweet. "It's not as if I opened it myself," she said, and began to nibble.

She nibbled her way into the packet and found a marzipan pig. "Lovely," said the mouse, and ate up the pig. The pig was fresh from the confectioner's

and had no experience of life whatever. There was
not a single thought in him, just marzipan. The
mouse was tired from the morning's hurly-burly,
and the sweetness made her drowsy. She fell asleep
inside the brown-paper packet.

The little boy who lived at No. 6 came to the
letter basket and saw the packet. That day was his
birthday and the packet had his name on it.
"Perhaps it's another marzipan pig from Aunt
Constantia," he said. He saw the hole in one corner
of the packet. "Perhaps someone's been here before
me," he said.

He opened the packet. The tearing of the paper woke the mouse. She sprang out of the packet, leapt to the floor, and ran into the nearest hole in the skirting-board.

As the mouse sat there breathing hard, she heard the boy's mother call from the kitchen, "Any letters?"

"Three for you and one for Dad," said the boy, "and a mouse in a pink frock for me but she ran off."

"A mouse in a pink frock!" said his mother.

"Maybe she wanted to be a hibiscus," said the boy.

"Not any more," said the mouse as she sat behind the skirting-board. She did not take off her hibiscus-petal frock though. She went out that evening and did not get eaten by the owl. She was seen at three o'clock in the morning dancing on the Embankment by the Albert Bridge.

Some other Puffins

FRYING AS USUAL
Joan Lingard

Disaster strikes the Francettis when Mr Francetti breaks his leg. Their fish and chip shop never closes, but who is going to run it now that's he's in hospital and their mother is in Italy? The answer is quite simple to Toni, Rosita and Paula, and with the help of Grandpa they decide to carry on frying as usual. But it's not that easy . . .

THE FREEDOM MACHINE
Joan Lingard

Mungo dislikes Aunt Janet and to avoid staying with her he decides to hit the open road and look after himself, and with his bike he heads northwards bound for adventure and freedom. But he soon discovers that freedom isn't quite what he'd expected, especially when his food supplies are stolen, and in the course of his journey he learns a few things about himself.

RACSO AND THE RATS OF NIMH
Jane Leslie Conly

When fieldmouse Timothy Frisby rescues young Racso, the city rat, from drowning it's the beginning of a friendship and an adventure. The two are caught up in the struggle of the Rats of NIMH to save their home from destruction. A powerful sequel to MRS FRISBY AND THE RATS OF NIMH.

NICOBOBINUS
Terry Jones

Nicobobinus and his friend, Rosie, find themselves in all sorts of intriguing adventures when they set out to find the Land of the Dragons long ago. Stunningly illustrated by Michael Foreman.

TUMBLEWEED

Dick King-Smith

Sir Tumbleweed is tall and thin with bright red hair and a droopy moustache. Not surprisingly, life in merrie England is pretty dull for this ordinary knight when he's so nervous and accident-prone – he practically trips over his own suit of armour! But the flattering attentions of an evil-looking witch, a lion and a unicorn change his life and before he knows what's happening he has floored Sir Basil the Beastly in a jousting match!

MR MOON'S LAST CASE

Brian Patten

Mr Moon is old and tired. He's had enough of this life but he still believes in magic. Something stirs in his soul when he hears there have been reported sightings of a strange, child-sized being, called a leprechaun by the press, and he decides he must track it down. A long journey begins, and as his obsession with finding the creature grows, he is carried to the brink of fairy-land itself.

MYSTERIES OF THE SEALS

Rosalind Kerven

All the fish have disappeared from the waters around the Scottish fishing village where Tom and Katie live. There is something sinister happening. The men have all been laid off and the whole village seems to be falling asleep – it's almost as if someone has put an evil spell on the place.

BOY and GOING SOLO

Roald Dahl

The enthralling autobiography of this much-loved author, from his earliest days to his experiences as a pilot in the Second World War.

THE APPRENTICES

Leon Garfield

A collection of the much-acclaimed Apprentices stories. Each story features one London trade and is linked by recurring characters.

THE BONNY PIT LADDIE

Frederick Grice

Set in the early twentieth century, this story of a boy growing up in a mining village was one of the first children's books to show real working-class children in credible surroundings.

SARAH, PLAIN AND TALL

Patricia MacLachlan

What would she be like, this new mother found through a newspaper advertisement? And above all, would she be able to sing?

STORM BIRD

Elsie McCutcheon

Torn from her father and her London school, Jenny is sent to live with her grim and sometimes frightening aunt in a small East Anglian seaside town. She is befriended by Josh, son of her aunt's wealthy employer, and shares his secret, passionate interest in birds. But the sinister mystery of her aunt's past begins to haunt Jenny, as it does the whole village. As the web of horror and tragedy is unravelled, Jenny and Josh are thrown together in a gripping climax to this powerful and dramatic story.

MOONDIAL

Helen Cresswell

Minty has heard stories of strange happenings in the big house across the road from her Aunt's cottage. And when she walks through the gates, the lodge-keeper knows it is Minty who holds the key to the mysteries. She has only to discover the secret power of the moondial, and she will be ready to carry out the dangerous mission which awaits her . . .

A haunting and beautifully written time-travel novel, by the author of *The Secret World of Polly Flint*.

TALES FOR THE TELLING

Edna O'Brien

In *Tales for the Telling* you'll meet giants and leprechauns, heroes and princesses. Stories of love and high deeds which have been passed from generation to generation are now presented together in this colourful and charming volume. A huge tradition of Irish storytelling is now available to a new audience.